Dedicated with love to my aunt,

Sally Clark Sloop

Thank you for showing me how much
fun it is to create stories
out of a single spark of inspiration.

I love you and I hope you enjoy
reading this with your grandchildren!

D0920449

Table of Contents

Chapter 1
My Adventures

Last summer I backpacked through Europe for six weeks. I saw places I had always dreamed of visiting. I toured ancient castles, saw famous monuments, and admired priceless art in world-renowned museums. I climbed narrow spiral stairs in bell towers and walked for hours along the cobbled streets of old cities. I soaked in as many new experiences as I could fit into each long summer day. I met and talked with interesting people from multiple countries, but by far, the most memorable friend I made was an elderly Italian woman with beautiful jet black hair named Luna.

I first learned about Luna in a magazine article. She was pictured in her olive grove and quoted as an expert on olive oil. She had such a unique appearance and a fun twinkle in her eye, I knew my travels would be incomplete without meeting her. I searched for her address on the internet, but I could not find it. Hoping to find her I bought a train ticket to her town. Fortunately, as soon as I stepped off the train I saw a sign for her business.

I followed a series of these simple signs until I reached a large stone house with a gated garden.

When I arrived Luna was softly humming a mesmerizing tune while tending large tomato plants in her garden. "*Buongiorno,* good morning Signora Luna," I said softly, not wanting to startle her. "I am eager to taste the best olive oil this side of Venice. May I come in please, *per favore?*"

"*Sì, sì, sì, yes!*" she enthusiastically answered while motioning for me to enter the garden gate. "Taste it you will! *Entra per favore,* come in please. My olive oil is the best in this land! It is best enjoyed with good food. Good food is best enjoyed with good wine. Good wine is best enjoyed with a good story!"

With her enticing invitation, I was instantly filled with delight and curiosity. I was about to make a new friend I would never forget and hear a story I would still be retelling when I am old.

Chapter 2
The Olive Grove

A long time ago in northern Italy in the month of May, Mario was hungry and in need of work. He walked kilometer after kilometer, village after village, through the foothills of the Dolomite Mountains searching for good fortune. Mario was a very lazy man. His laziness caused him to lose a series of jobs, but he was also a very superstitious man. He believed his hardships were the result of breaking a mirror four years ago.

Mario's wealthy aunt who lived on the Grand Canal in Venice gave him the mirror for his birthday when he was a boy. In his teenage years, he admired himself in the mirror for hours every day as he dreamed about a bright future. But as his life became more and more unsettled, he struggled to be hopeful. He was convinced he had at least three more years of bad luck ahead of him before he would escape the curse of the broken mirror.

Mario trudged along filled with bitterness and anger as he recollected his many lost jobs over the years. He was so grouchy when he entered a new village, he did not offer customary greetings such as *"Buongiorno."* Instead he loudly announced, "I need someone to give me a job chopping wood, carrying water, or tending goats." Women hurried inside their homes and children hid when they heard his deep, bellowing, angry voice.

By Mario's fourth week of jobless searching, he was thin and exhausted. His broad shoulders sagged as he trudged onward cursing under his breath about his bad luck. His once young and handsome face, despite his rather large nose, grew angular from weight loss. His eyes even appeared smaller and less round because he glared angrily most of the time. His beard and mustache, brown with hints of red, were quite full. They could have been his best features, but they were unkempt. He saw his reflection from time to time in pools of water, but he no longer cared about his appearance as he once had.

Mario had almost given up hope of finding work and a better life when he saw a steep, narrow, rocky path one evening. The trail was unmarked, but he felt compelled to follow it for a reason he could not explain. He continued until the path ended at an olive grove. The olive trees were very well tended; they were all pruned in the same shape and to the same height of four meters. They grew in straight rows numbering thirteen in each row.

If Mario had counted the trees, he might not have entered the grove. He believed thirteen was an unlucky number, but he was too tired after a long day of walking to pay much attention to detail. The ground was covered in soft grass. Wild peonies and irises bloomed along the inside border of the perimeter stone wall. It was a lovely place. Mario, however, only saw it as a resting place for one night before continuing on his journey the next morning. As the sun disappeared behind the mountain and the colors of the evening sky faded into darkness, Mario reclined under a tree. He quickly fell into a fitful, hungry sleep.

Early the next morning, he woke to the constant calling of cuckoo birds on the mountain. "*Cuckoo... cuckoo...cuckoo*," sang the birds back and forth to one another. "*Basta! Basta!* Stop! I'll never get back to sleep with your noise!" he yelled. Frustrated and irritated, he slowly and stiffly rose, twisting and arching his broad aching back as he stood. "Maybe today will be my lucky day?" he grumbled.

He picked a handful of small olives and greedily ate them. They were hard and bitter. Olives are not ripe until autumn, but he was famished so he ate them anyway. Then he had more. He cursed loudly as he chewed the disgusting olives. "*Basta! Basta! Basta!*" he shouted again toward the persistent birds while spitting bits of olives from his mouth. "Can't a man have breakfast in peace?" His booming voice echoed off the mountain like thunder.

Unsatisfied with the olives, Mario climbed a tree hoping to find a bird's nest full of eggs or to spy something else more palatable to eat. Unfortunately, all he discovered was a large spider's web. He exploded with rage as the dewy web stuck instantly in his bushy mustache and knotted beard. As he furiously batted his face to remove the sticky web, the branch supporting him cracked.

With a loud snap the limb broke and fell, and so did Mario. Tree branches scratched him as he fell. One branch scraped across his right eye and deeply cut him from his cheek to his forehead. He was fortunate the branch did not injure his eye, but Mario felt anything but grateful.

He lay across the broken branch bleeding. He crossly wondered how his day could get any worse when he suddenly noticed a short woman a meter away.

She stood on the opposite side of the low, white stone wall with one hand on her hip and the other on a long wooden staff. She peered intently and curiously at Mario with her sparkling dark eyes. Mario stared back startled by her sudden arrival and confused by her contrasting features. He was not sure if she was a young woman or an old woman. She had long wavy black hair that flowed over her shoulders and down her back in a youthful way, but her face and hands were extremely wrinkled.

Chapter 3
Breakfast

Tu chi sei? Who are you?" the woman asked.

"*Io sono Mario.* I am Mario," he grunted, still dazed from his fall and surprised by the sudden appearance of the odd woman. "I am hungry and I need work."

"Work indeed you will!" the woman said in a high-pitched, but authoritative voice. "You trespassed on my land, ate my olives, and broke one of my finest trees," she exclaimed as she held up a crooked finger on one hand and decisively tapped her long staff on the wall. She knew Mario had eaten her olives because bits of olives clung to his beard.

"*Io sono Luna,*" she continued. "When I was a young woman, I planted these trees. I have cared for my friends, these olive trees, meticulously for many moons. They are very valuable to me. Their fruit gives me the best *olio d'olvia*, olive oil from here to Venice. It is how I earn a living. Now, you have damaged Luigi, the father of all of my trees. You have also spoiled this beautiful, peaceful morning with your yelling."

Mario sat up, continuing to stare at the old woman with a puzzled expression on his bleeding face. He did not know what to think of her. She was odd for sure! Not only did she have an unusual appearance, but she named trees, and she seemed to arrive to the grove out of thin air. He also thought she was very bossy, and he did not like to be told what to do. *How dare this little old woman talk to me as if I am a child?* he thought.

Mario gritted his yellowed teeth and grunted in pain as he stood up to reveal his great height to the petite woman. Hoping to intimidate her and stop her chatter, he looked with a nasty glare down at Luna. Luna, however, continued to give instructions, not at all scared of Mario, who was almost twice her height.

"You will carry stones from the mountain stream and build this wall high enough that no one will ever be able to trespass into my grove or disturb my special trees again," she continued. "In exchange for your work, I will feed you. After all, you need food to have enough energy to build my wall." Mario's stomach growled, and his mouth watered at the mention of food.

"You are in luck. I am a good cook," Luna remarked proudly. She turned away and started to descend the path. "*Vieni adesso*, come now," she called over her shoulder to Mario who was still stunned from falling. "You can wash your face in the water pump while I prepare breakfast. Once we have eaten, you will return here and start building the wall."

Though not pleased to be ordered by a strange old woman, Mario was too enchanted by her promise of food to complain. They walked slowly due to the steep and rocky terrain. The path was not difficult for young Mario, but Luna steadied herself with her spiraled olive wood staff to keep from falling.

Bored with the slow pace, Mario stared at the walking stick. The wood was rich with many hues of brown and smooth from use over many years. Arrays of dark lines twisted and curved upward joining together at the rounded top of the staff. Mario had not eaten a decent meal in over a week. He felt dizzy as he stared at the patterns.   He blinked and forced himself to look away so he would not trip or fall.

Roughly twenty minutes later Luna and Mario crossed a field covered in poppies. Mario saw a very small house with wooden shutters and a young spring garden.

As they approached the house, Mario saw hens strutting in the yard. He drooled at the sight of the chickens. He patted his aching stomach and hoped Luna had enough food to satisfy him. If not, he promptly decided to sneak back in the night and steal a chicken or two.

"*Entra*. Come in," Luna said from the threshold of her one-room house as a black cat wound between her feet.

No, no!" exclaimed Mario as he staggered away from the door. "*Un gatto nero*, a black cat, is very bad luck! I have had enough bad luck already!"

Luna shook her head and smiled down at the cat, who looked back up at her with a slow blink as if she understood they were talking about her. "Nonsense," Luna said. "This cat is not bad luck at all. She is quite the opposite; a very special and lucky cat! You can wash your face over there at the pump. I will cook breakfast. You are in luck, my hens laid many eggs this morning."

"*Bene*, good," Mario grunted. "Luck is what I need." He walked backward to the water pump so he could keep an eye on the cat.

Mario pumped the water handle vigorously several times. The water was cold and refreshing. The long scratch across his right eye was not bleeding anymore. It would scar, but he did not care. What he did care about was making sure the cat did not cross his path. He looked around the little yard for a seat where he could watch the cat. Next to a humongous pile of large round stones at the edge of the garden, there was a short stack of neatly cut stones. Mario sat on the short sturdy stack facing the door where the cat remained looking back at him. Impatient for breakfast, and increasingly nervous because of the watchful cat, Mario tapped his foot and chewed on his fingernails.

Luna swiftly busied herself in the kitchen. She loved to entertain guests. Her first impression of Mario was not a good one, but she pitied him for he did seem extremely hungry. *Anyone hungry enough to eat unripe olives must be nearly starved to death*, she thought. *My cooking will be good for him. Perhaps he will be more pleasant after he has had a proper breakfast.* She hummed happily while she cracked eggs and hung a pot of water over the fire in the hearth.

Meanwhile, the cat continued to watch Mario with its bright yellow eyes from the doorway. Mario in return, glowered back at the cat. He was too edgy to look away, so he was quite surprised when Luna suddenly appeared next to him with a large platter of steaming polenta and fried eggs.

"I see you are interested in Fortuna, my cat. You should introduce yourself," she said with a playful laugh.

"How did you get out here? he asked bewildered. I have been watching that cat in the open door this whole time. I did not see you come out! Surely, there is another door?" *I will have to pay better attention*, he thought. *This is the second time this morning she has startled me.* Mario felt nervous, but his nerves were quickly eased by the sight of the generous plate of food Luna was holding.

"*Allora,*" sighed Luna with a modest smile as she handed him breakfast. "Never mind me or my little cat. *Vieni adesso*, let us sit under the persimmon tree and eat before the food is cold.

Mario held the plate under his large nose and inhaled deeply. The food smelled glorious. He buried his face in it and greedily gulped down three eggs and a heaping portion of polenta twice the size of his fist.

Disapproving of her guest's table manners, Luna shook her head at Mario. *I know he is extremely hungry, but good heavens, he eats like a pig*, she thought with disgust. "Slow down and use your manners young Mario! And wipe your beard and use your fork. Please remember your manners when you eat with me," she commanded. "*Allora*, now my appetite is ruined." Luna sighed and shook her head again.

Too transfixed by the delicious food to care that Luna was bossing him again, Mario obeyed. As he wiped orange egg yolk from his beard with the back of his hand, he said with a mouthful, "Your food is good. If you are not going to eat, give me your plate." After a loud swallow and an even louder belch, he grumbled, "*per favore?*" With the addition of "please," Luna passed her untouched breakfast to her poorly mannered guest.

Chapter 4
The Voice

"Now that I have fed you, you must work," Luna instructed Mario. "Walk back up the path. When you reach my olive trees turn left. You will find a stream in the woods. Collect one hundred large stones and carry them back to my olive grove. Stack them on the wall. If you complete this task before the sun sinks behind the mountain, I will feed you dinner."

"Hmmm," Mario replied stroking his long beard and thinking already about the possibility of more good food. "What you ask sounds extremely exhausting. I will need meat for dinner tonight to replenish my energy after such hard work," he said greedily looking from Luna to the chickens then back to Luna again.

"*Molto bene*, very well, I can agree to that," Luna said with a conclusive nod. "Tonight we will have chicken for dinner. Now, please excuse me, I am going to take a nap. I am tired after climbing the path and cooking for you. I am an old woman after all."

Rubbing his satisfied stomach he stood. "I will be back tonight," he said. He turned to leave, but he stopped abruptly, almost tripping over Fortuna. "*Vai! Vai!* Leave, go away!" Mario shouted, but the cat stubbornly stayed exactly where she was until Luna called her softly.

"*Vieni qui mio piccolo gatto nero,* come here my little black cat. Let us nap together while Mario works."

"Huurumpf!" Mario replied as he crossed the garden past the pile of stones and rudely slammed the gate closed.

Mario climbed the hill all the while cursing to himself about his plan to also take a nap once he reached the shade of the olive trees. "Now that I have eaten, I will rest well," he said to himself. *I am lucky Luna is a good cook,* he happily thought. *My stomach is full for the first time in weeks and tonight I will have roasted chicken! Perhaps, I will think about moving stones later, but first I will rest.*

And he did.

Mario slept deeply for the first time in weeks. He dreamed of roasted chicken and vegetables.

Meanwhile, inside her modest house, Luna lay on her short bed under the window which faced the mountain. She called Fortuna to join her and patted the bed, "*Vieni mio gatto.* Let's enjoy a rest together." Fortuna promptly jumped up. She turned twice in a circle, kneaded the quilt with her front paws for a few moments, then curled into a tight ball in a patch of sunlight next to Luna's feet.

"*Grazie,* thank you, Fortuna. You will make my aching feet feel better." Before the cat drifted off into a nap, as cats do best, Luna whispered to her feline friend, "*Andrà tutto bene.*"

An hour later Luna woke and felt refreshed. She cleaned the kitchen and worked in the garden. She was happiest when she was outside. The sunshine energized her and made her feel youthful. She whistled, mimicking bird calls while she worked. Her whistles were so precise she often confused birds who came right up to her expecting another bird, not a petite human. Luna had lived her whole life on this *pedemonte,* foot of the mountain.   She knew the land and its secrets extremely well. What she had not learned from keen observations, she read in books passed down from her great-great-grandmother, Befana, who was a legendary *strega*, witch.

Today Luna staked tomato plants. Her tomatoes always grew quickly.   In a few weeks, they would need support as to not break under their own weight.   She delicately tied each young plant to a sturdy pole buried in the rich, but rocky soil.   She sang to the plants encouraging them to grow big and fruitful.

Mario on the other hand slept and slept. He slept all morning and into the afternoon.   He would have kept on sleeping, but an olive fell; landing exactly on the fresh scratch on his forehead.   "*Ahia*, ouch!" He yelled and cursed as he woke with a jerk.   "What was that?" He was not expecting an answer, but in his sleepy state, he thought he heard the reply, "It was me."

Mario did not hear anything else for several minutes.   He rolled to his side and fell back to sleep.   As he slept a voice spoke, "*Move the stones you will or else you will be still.*"   Mario heard the rhyme in his dreams.

The message was clearly a warning, and he shifted fitfully in his sleep.

When he woke, the bottom of the sun appeared to be touching the top of the mountain. He had slept all day. He yawned and stretched his back with a loud crack. "*Ahhh. My day started badly, but then I ate a good breakfast and enjoyed a long nap. Next I will have a good dinner. This is a lucky day after all! Maybe I will move stones tomorrow, if I feel like it. As for the old woman, she won't know I've been sleeping. She is too old to climb the hill twice in one day,*" he thought.

Mario glanced upward for a branch to pull himself up. When he did, he looked straight into a pair of yellow eyes.

"*Vai! Via!* Leave me alone!" he yelled at Fortuna who calmly sat on a low branch. Mario stood quickly and backed away putting distance between himself and the black cat. "My fortune has just started to change, but *you* will bring me bad luck!" he shouted. "*Vai, vai!*" Fortuna stretched her back into a high arch then slowly yawned revealing her sharp teeth. Without ever breaking eye contact with Mario, she slowly stepped with confidence toward him along a thin branch.

"AAAHHHHH!" he screamed as he stumbled backward nearly falling over an exposed tree root.

For a split second, Mario thought the cat was mocking him. *That's ridiculous*, he reassured himself. *It is only a cat; even if it is a black cat. I must not let my superstitions get the best of me.* Nevertheless, he felt nervous being so close to the cat because evening shadows were making it difficult to see her. He did not want her to come any closer to him.

Making sure Fortuna was not following him, he stepped backward again. By the time he stepped over the wall, all he could see of Fortuna were her eyes shining in the orange-pink glow of the fading sunset.

"I do not like that cat...not one bit," he muttered. He was anxious to leave the cat and eager to eat again. His stomach growled loudly as he descended the path. Gradually, he relaxed as he walked, forgetting about his encounter with the cat because images of roasted chicken filled his mind.

Mario reached Luna's garden gate just as the sun completely sank behind the mountain. The tiny house needed some repairs, but it looked inviting. A single candle flickered in the window, and smoke rose from the chimney. Mario had not enjoyed the luxury of meat in a long time, so he quickly crossed the yard having smelled the glorious aroma of roasted chicken!

"*Fantastico!*"

Chapter 5
The Chicken Dinner

Hearing Mario, Luna wiped her hands on her red apron and pushed her hair behind her ear. She stepped into the threshold to greet her guest. "*Buonasera*, good evening," she said pleasantly. Mario looked across the yard at her horrified. To his great surprise, the old woman was not alone! Fortuna sat upright in the doorway with her tail wrapped around her front paws as if she were guarding the door.

That cat almost looks like it is smiling at me, Mario thought. *I do not like that cat!* The calmness from his walk immediately vanished and was replaced by a mix of fear and anger. His eyes narrowed, his jaw tensed, and he shouted, "That cat! I just saw it in the olive grove! Now it is here? I do not like that cat! Tell it to go away. Black cats are very bad luck."

"Never you mind Fortuna," Luna reassured her nervous guest. "She is friendly to those who are also friendly. *Vieni adesso*, let us eat."

Holding her tail high, Fortuna sauntered into the yard past Mario. He took three steps to the side as she passed and held his breath as if that might ward off bad luck from the black cat. Once the cat was on the far side of the garden, Mario ducked his head and stepped through the low arched door. The room was sparsely decorated with a bed under the window, a small round table with two chairs, one of which needed repairs, a shelf with many large books, and a fireplace. Mario crossed the room in only three steps and loudly plopped down into the nicer chair. He tapped his foot with impatient hunger while Luna finished cooking.

Luna shook her head and bit her tongue keeping her opinions of Mario's manners to herself. She consulted a thick leather book, added final spices to the chicken, and removed a heavy copper pot from the fire. She was humming the same tune from breakfast as she handed Mario a heaping plate of hot roasted chicken and poured two glasses of wine from a ceramic chicken pitcher.

Without hesitation, Mario picked up a chicken leg with both hands and began to eat. "You..must really…like…chickens," he commented between rapid, loud bites as chicken juices glistened on his lips and dripped into his tangled beard. The meat was tender and savory, seasoned perfectly with fresh rosemary and thyme from Luna's garden. It was the most succulent meat Mario had ever tasted. *What good fortune I've had to meet a good cook*, he thought. Already finished with the drumstick, Mario began devouring another piece. Luna was still serving her own plate.

She strongly disapproved of her guest's poor manners, but she once again chose to ignore his rudeness. She was too hungry to waste time rebuking Mario. After all, this morning he ate her breakfast. She sat with a quiet sigh then answered, "*Sì, sì, sì,* I do like chickens. You know, legend says a chicken pitcher will protect a home from danger. The chicken we are eating was my friend, just as my olive trees are my friends.   I take good care of my land and my chickens. They are good to me and provide me food and income. But of all of my friends, my cat is most special to me."

Mario was too engrossed in his meal to listen carefully.   He had no idea what the old woman was saying. Something about special animals was all he heard. He was completely enraptured by the delicious meat. Mario greedily wondered what other foods Luna could cook well. *Perhaps I should stay on the hill through the summer while the weather is nice and eat her cooking every day,* he pondered. *She will never know if I am building the wall or not. Surely she will not hike up to the grove for a long time…it's too hard of a hike, especially for an old woman!*

Luna ate a small sensible meal. She finished before Mario, who for the second time in one day stuffed himself with all of the remaining food. Since Mario was not much for conversation, much less conversation interesting to Luna, she quietly rose and poured herself another glass of wine. As she stood, Mario suddenly stopped his loud chewing mid-bite because he heard a soft voice drifting in from the open window. It was hard to discern the words, but it seemed vaguely familiar. He listened closely tilting his chair back to lean toward the window behind him.

"Move the stones you will, or else you will be still."

Mario rubbed his eyes and shook his head to clear his ears. Surely, being around this odd little woman and her sneaky cat, had his imagination running wild!

What in the world was that? And who could be out there? I have not seen another person in two days walk, he thought.

The mysterious voice had a pleasant tone, but Mario was nervous. He could not imagine who, or worse what could be talking. With increasing anxiety, he glanced at Luna to see her reaction, but she seemed perfectly at ease. *Perhaps her hearing is poor, and she did not hear what I think I heard,* he reasoned.

Luna heard the rhyme too, but it did not surprise or even alarm her. She knew it was Fortuna's voice they were hearing. A few years ago, while Luna was collecting mushrooms in the forest, she found a tiny, weak, black kitten. She carried the kitten home in her apron pocket, fed it goat's milk, and cared for it tenderly. The kitten grew into a beautiful, sleek cat with a long tail and long black whiskers. She followed Luna everywhere and seemed to pay close attention to all of Luna's chores. The young cat was so attentive and so curious, Luna knew she was highly intelligent. Wishing she knew what her furry friend was thinking and longing for a companion with whom to converse,

Luna consulted Befana's books. She was determined to find a way for Fortuna to speak.

Several months passed, but Luna perfected a concoction of herbs that when eaten enabled the cat to speak. In the first words Fortuna spoke, she expressed her gratitude to Luna for rescuing her as a kitten and giving her a good home. After that the two friends talked about everything. They already shared Luna's bed and meals together, but now they were able to share their talents. Luna taught the young cat many fables. Fortuna taught Luna to move from place to place undetected as a black cat can do best.

Now, hearing Fortuna's sweet voice in the garden, Luna smiled and pretended to be oblivious to the sound of the rhyme floating in again on the night breeze. Luna turned around and saw Mario sitting on the edge of his chair with an open mouth and wide eyes. He had stopped eating mid-bite.

"Did you say something?" he nervously stuttered. He was anxious to leave the little house despite Luna's excellent cooking. *Luna is odd the way she names her trees and talks to her cat, but that voice is eerie. Maybe I should leave now? I don't need any more bad luck*, he thought. Mario trembled and the hair on the back of his neck tingled.

"No, not I," said Luna in a deliberately calm voice. "Perhaps you are just tired from a long day of moving stones." She knew Mario had slept all day in the olive grove because Fortuna had told her, but she did not reveal this knowledge.

"*Sì*, that must be it," he said trying to convince himself he had not heard anything. "Or maybe I drank too much of your wine. I must go to sleep now so I will have the energy to move stones again tomorrow," he lied. Mario abruptly slid the chair back from the table. It scraped across the wood floor making a horrible noise. Mario jumped at the sound.

"*Buonanotte* Mario, good night," said Luna. "Tomorrow you may come again, and I will share my good food in exchange for your work adding one hundred more stones to the wall before the sun sets behind the mountain."

"*Sì, sì, sì. Domani,* tomorrow," he replied, greedily thinking about his next free meal and hoping he was overreacting about the voice outside.

Chapter 6

Patience

Luna woke at first light the next morning. Fortuna was curled in a tight circle next to her hip. Luna patted then scratched her head gently waking her. "*Grazie*, you know my favorite spots," Fortuna dreamily said with a soft purr.

Luna sat up, reached across the little bed, and opened the shutters. *I really must concoct something to help me see clearly all the way to the top of the hill*, she thought. *I could save Fortuna from traveling to the grove. Alora, I will read in my books about improving my distance vision. It is just not as sharp as it was when I was younger.* After a few minutes she spied Mario at the foot of the path.

As he got closer, Luna noticed he looked tired and grouchy, even more grouchy than the previous day. His mouth was turned down in a sour frown and he had dark circles under his eyes like the lids of cast iron pots. "*Vieni adesso* Fortuna, let us prepare breakfast. I do not think Mario will be any more pleasant this morning than he was yesterday, but perhaps we will soften him with our company and good cooking."

Fortuna stood, stretching her front legs forward with her head tucked down and her hips high. She yawned before replying, "You are more patient than I am Luna. I would not feed him one more bite. He is lazy and will cause us trouble! He did not keep his part of the agreement yesterday, and he lied about it."

"You are correct my little cat, but Mario deserves a chance to make good choices. We will wait and see. *Andrà tutto bene*, everything will be fine. I have a plan."

Mario shoved open the garden gate and yelled, "I could barely sleep last night! That cat of yours came to the grove. Half the night I could hear it in the trees above me. When I did sleep, I had terrible dreams about talking cats. Have you ever heard anything so ridiculous?"

Luna laughed as if to agree with Mario, but she was actually giggling because she knew he had not dreamed about a talking cat at all! Fortuna noiselessly entered the grove around midnight while Mario snored. She recited fables for several hours then returned home in enough time for a cat nap before dawn. Luna winked quickly at Fortuna. "*Vieni adesso* Mario. Let us eat so you will have enough strength to build my wall."

Mario greedily ate scrambled eggs and thick slices of tomato, which were almost as wide as the plate itself. When he finished, he left without thanking Luna for breakfast. Once he was away from the yard, Fortuna said, "His manners revolt me. A cat would never eat so much so quickly or with such a mess! A cat would always show gratitude also. *Perché*, why are you letting him continue as our guest?"

Luna smiled knowingly at Fortuna and patted her lap for the cat to come and sit. She slowly stroked the cat's silky black fur to calm her as she explained the rhyme to Fortuna detailing what would happen if Mario continued to break their agreement. "Be patient my little cat and give him time. We shall see what kind of man Mario truly is. We will wait, a*spettiamo qui piccolo gatto mio.*"

Chapter 7
The Summer

Each morning Mario walked down the hill for breakfast then back up to the grove. At the end of each day he walked down the hill again and enjoyed Luna's good food. He repeated this pattern for nearly four months. Between meals, he mostly lounged and napped. The grove remained his favorite resting place because the grass was soft. There were relatively few rocks compared to the forest floor which was littered with white stones of all sizes. When the weather was especially hot, he wandered into the forest to sit by the stream. The cold, rushing water from the mountain high above cooled the air enough that Mario could rest comfortably. On the hottest days, he bathed in the stream and occasionally he washed his clothes. But washing days were few and far between. Most days, he did not accomplish anything.

Fortuna also went to the grove daily to observe Mario's routine and to see if he had moved any stones. His laziness irritated her, but she kept her promise to Luna to be patient.

Early in the summer, Mario actually had a few honorable intentions. "*Domani, domani,* I will move the stones," he said to himself as he lounged idly in the shade. But as the summer progressed he thought more often of how lucky he was to have free food than he did of working. *I have tricked her well,* he thought with devious delight. He was convinced Luna did not know about his daily routine. She had not returned to the grove since the morning they met. He was pleased with himself, and he was also very pleased with Luna's good food. He did not even feel guilty about resting all day long because the hike up and down the hill twice a day in the heat did tire him. The steep walk was also becoming more strenuous for Mario. He was gaining weight rapidly.

Mario's complacency about his agreement grew almost as fast as his bulging stomach! As the summer days became shorter, he hardly ever thought about his agreement to build the wall. He thought more and more about his good fortune. He believed the curse of the broken mirror ended prematurely. "I am a lucky man now," he said to himself each morning as he woke.

He was completely satisfied with life, except for Fortuna. Her presence unnerved him. She seemed to be everywhere he was. He especially did not like it when she startled him. At least once a day she snuck up on him without making any sound. He still believed black cats were bad luck, but everything was going so well, he tried to ignore Fortuna.

As for Luna, when she was not cooking or reading, she spent hours a day happily working in her garden. Tomatoes, beans, zucchini, and greens flourished with her attention. She was an exceptional gardener, but she also used a secret fertilizer from one of Befana's books to make the vegetables grow more plentifully.

Each month on the night of the full moon, she mixed equal parts of moon and fairy dust. The powder sparkled like diamonds on the ground before it slowly dissolved into the soil. Together with her natural green thumb and the fertilizer, the garden produced plenty of vegetables, especially tomatoes, to store for the winter despite how much Mario ate daily.

The garden was not the only area of Luna's yard growing. The short stack of cut stones was growing higher. Luna and Fortuna were both pleased with the increasing height of the wall. If Mario noticed the changes, he never mentioned it to Luna. Twice a day when he entered the garden gate, the aromas of Luna's good cooking enraptured him, and he thought only of food.

Chapter 8

The Stones

By late September when the persimmons on Luna's tree changed from yellow to orange, Mario no longer believed in the value of working for a living. *Why work at all when I can eat for free?* Knowing the old woman would eventually come to the olive grove, he thought again of what to say. *The work is difficult. I require help or more time to build the wall high enough to protect from intruders.*

Luna also knew the time to return to the grove was drawing near. Fortuna agreed. "The olives are ripe for harvest. Are you ready Luna?"

"*Sì, sì, sì,*" she replied with a smile as she patted Fortuna's head. "I will give him two more days. Please warn him again."

Early the next morning in the dark, Fortuna navigated the steep path. She climbed up a tree and perched high above the fat, lazy, snoring man. *You should listen to me!*

"*Move the stones you will, or else you will be still.*"

Mario woke with fright. He frantically looked side to side for the source of the voice, but he was unsuccessful. Fortuna was well hidden by dense branches at the top of the tree. Her high position was not necessary. If Mario had seen her, he would not suspect a cat of speaking, but Fortuna loved to be up high. She also knew treetops were the best places to enjoy a sunrise.

Mario heard the rhyme clearly this time. He thought back to when he first heard it in the spring. *What could it mean? And who is speaking?* he wondered. He wrestled with the meaning of the rhyme well into the morning, but then tired from waking before dawn, he fell asleep. In the middle of the afternoon, he woke. He was very hungry because he had slept through breakfast. He walked to Luna's house earlier than usual. As soon as he smelled her good cooking, he once again forgot about the worrisome voice.

"*Buonasera,* Mario. You have dined with me through four moons now. My olives are ready to harvest. *Domani* I will come to the grove and inspect your progress on the wall. Why it must be higher than the roof of my little house by now!" Luna knowingly proclaimed.

Instantly, Mario's face grew red hot. Tomorrow Luna would discover his idleness and she might make him leave this gluttonous life of leisure. A moral man would feel guilty about breaking an agreement, but Mario was not a moral man. He was entitled, dishonest and lackadaisical. As he silently ate his breakfast he thought again of what to tell Luna. *I will move stones today. Then I can honestly explain what hard work it is. If she truly wants a high wall to protect her grove from intruders she will need a big man like me to complete the work. I bet I can convince her to let me stay longer.*

Moving the stones was hard work! It was more difficult than any work Mario had ever attempted. He tired quickly and was completely exhausted after moving only seven stones from the stream to the wall. In May he was lean, but strong. Now after a summer of eating and sleeping, he was round and weak. The work truly was too difficult for him. He sat against a tree to catch his breath. In no time he was snoring like a bear. He was so exhausted, he slept straight through dinner and all night long.

The next morning, harvest day, Mario woke to find Luna standing over him. She looked down at him and shook her head at him, but she did not speak right away. Mario did not speak either.

Fortuna was also silent. She sat on top of one of the seven new stones Mario added to the wall the day before. Her head was cocked to one side and she stared at Mario. *I warned you, Mario, and Luna gave you plenty of chances,* she thought. Mario had the impression the cat was laughing at him.

"*Buongiorno* Mario," Luna finally said. She paused because she was a little breathless from her hike. She leaned on her staff and continued, "I have come to see my friends, the olive trees, and to inspect your progress with my wall. Now, I see that the olives have grown ripe, but the wall has only grown higher in this one small section. I generously fed you twice every day, but you have not worked as we agreed many moons ago."

Mario began to utter excuses, but the voice interrupted him. Having moved stealthily to a low branch centimeters above Mario's head, Fortuna stated the rhyme, *"Move the stones you will, or else you will be still."*

Realizing the voice was directly above him, Mario rolled his eyes upward meeting Fortuna's confident gaze. Her bright eyes sparkled in the morning light. Mario felt petrified being so close to her. When he saw her mouth move in speech, he screamed.

"AAAAAAAHHHHHHH!"

He screamed so loudly all of the birds within many kilometers flew away. He screamed and wildly waved his arms above his head. He wanted to be as far away from Luna and her spine-chilling cat as his fat legs could carry him. Disoriented and frightened out of his wits, he ran frantically through the grove toward the forest and staggered clumsily over the low stone wall. He only ran a few meters into the rocky forest before he tripped on a stone. Luna raised her olive wood staff. At the precise moment he fell to the ground in a heap, she commanded, *"Essere ancora!* Be still!"

And he was.

Mario stiffened and turned to stone.

"*Bene, bene!*" cheered Fortuna happily, "Well done Luna! We are finally rid of him!"

Luna sighed with relief, smiled, and lovingly scratched behind Fortuna's ear. "*Grazie* for supervising Mario this summer and repeatedly warning him."

"*Prego*, you are welcome Luna."

"We were generous and merciful to Mario all summer. He had many chances to honor our agreement, but alas, he did not. I promised you all would be well for us didn't I?"

"*Sì*, you did Luna."

"*Vieni gatto mio*, let us walk home and enjoy a peaceful breakfast together before we harvest the olives. You were correct Fortuna, the olives are ready. Our trees have given us an exceptional harvest this year! I think we will earn enough money from olive oil sales this season to build a proper *fogolar friulano*, hearth in our new house. It will be perfect for keeping us warm in winter and for cooking good food for us and our guests.

"*Sì, sì, sì*, Luna, that sounds wonderful. *Andrà tutu bene!* Our new house is progressing well too. I look forward to living with you in it for years to come. I do have one request though. In the future can we welcome only nice guests *per favore?*"

Luna giggled lovingly at Fortuna's request. She reached up in the tree and gently picked up her friend. Holding her close to her heart she replied, "*Molto bene,* I can agree to that. Perhaps in our new house we should have a new rule. Do you think '*be nice or leave*' will work well?"

"*Perfetto!*" purred Fortuna.

Chapter 9
My Wonder

"Mario, of course, was never seen nor heard from again in all of Italy. For good reasons, no one, especially Fortuna, ever missed him," Luna said with a smile as she pet a black cat who had settled on her lap half way through the story.

"Wow, what a fun story! You are a marvelous storyteller Signora Luna. You are also an excellent cook! I especially loved *la bruschetta al pomodoro*, tomato toast. And you were correct, your olive oil, food, wine and the story, are the perfect combination for a wonderful afternoon! *Grazie mille*, thank you very much for entertaining me," I said having finished a plate of delectable appetizers and many samples of delicious olive oil.

"*Prego*, you are welcome," replied Luna satisfied with my delight.

"Please, tell me how you came to have such a large house? In your story, your home was quite small."

"*Allora*, how could I forget that part? Over that summer long, long ago, while Mario slept at night in the olive grove, the round stones in my yard from years of gardening this rocky soil transformed into perfectly cut building stones. One stone changed for every stone Mario neglected to move. Then, using the power of levitation of course, for I am an old woman and cannot lift stones on my own, I stacked them to build a new house."

"I see," I replied politely though I did not believe her explanation.

"Mario's laziness turned out well for me and my cat after all. It took me many years to complete my new house because even with magic moving stones is very hard work, but time has always been on my side," she said with a quick wink. "Now, I have lived here for several thousand moons." Luna winked at me playfully.

"That is a long time," I said politely as I started to calculate how many years equaled one thousand moon cycles. But Luna, who must have sensed my puzzlement, interrupted my calculations by handing me another spoonful of golden olive oil to sample.

"I'm very pleased you like my story and my oil. Indeed, it is good for your health! Furthermore, your hair will always be beautiful like mine if you swallow two spoonfuls a day," she said. The black cat stretched and sat up. It cocked its head and stared intently at me. "Now, how many bottles of oil will you purchase today?"

I shook my head slightly and blinked to break eye contact with the cat. "This truly is the best olive oil I have tasted since I arrived in Italy. I would like three bottles please," I answered my hostess. "I wish I could purchase more, but I think three bottles is all I can fit in my backpack. Can I order on-line once I get home?"

"Good heavens, no!" Luna said with a laugh. "If you desire more of my special oil, you must return to Italy and visit me again. I have no use for the internet or computers. I prefer to entertain my customers in person, just as I have entertained you."

"Well then Signora Luna, I hope I will be able to return to Italy and visit you again."

"*Sarò qui*, I will be here," she replied with a wink.

I paid for the oil and thanked Luna again for her hospitality. "*Arrivederci e buonanotte*, good-bye and good night Signora Luna," I said as I gently closed the garden gate. She smiled and waved to me as the cat wound between her feet.

Luna walked toward the large stone house and I walked up the road. Before I turned at a bend in the road, I looked back for one last look at the house where I had just enjoyed the most memorable afternoon of my adventures. When I did, I saw the house resembled a man with small dark eyes, a long broad nose, and a bushy mustache. There was even a vertical bar in the top right window just like the scar on Mario's face. I stared in wonder. Perhaps my imagination was getting the best of me. Or perhaps I had enjoyed too much good wine, but to me, the front of the house looked exactly like Luna's description of Mario!

How curious, I thought. *I wonder if she made up the story because of the appearance of her house? Or maybe her story is true? Could Luna really have magical powers? Could she really be as old as she claims? I don't know, but I like her nonetheless!* My mind raced with impossible questions.

By this time, there was a beautiful orange glow on the mountain from the setting sun and the rising full moon. I wanted to explore more before it was too dark to see well. I took a picture of the house and instantly wished I had taken a picture with Luna too.

"*Oh well,*" I thought, "*maybe next time. I do hope there*

is a next time!" Filled with hope of a future visit with Luna, I continued around the corner and up the steep road.

After I walked about half of a kilometer, I discovered a very old olive grove. It must have been Luna's grove. The trees, twisted and gnarled as olive trees are, stood trimmed to the same height and in straight rows with thirteen trees per row. A low stone wall surrounded the grove. The wall, however, in contrast to the trees, was in disrepair and almost completely covered in ivy. *I don't know if Luna's story of Mario is just a fun fable to entertain her guests or if parts of it are true, but her message about trespassing and honesty was very clear.* I dared not enter the grove or into the woods beyond. I did not want to be disrespectful or cause any trouble.

And because I saw a black cat sitting at the top of an olive tree. It looked straight at me with bright yellow eyes.

Fine
The End

The Mario House

A house in my neighborhood village built in the 1700s.
The *fogolar friulano* is in the room under Mario's
mustache.

Luna's *Fogolar Friulano*

The *fogolar* is still operational today, but it is no longer the primary heating or cooking source for the house.

Luna's Olive Grove

An old olive grove through the woods and up a steep narrow path from my house.
(But there are only twelve trees in each row.)

Un Pò,
A Little Bit About the
Italian References:

Italy:

Italia or Italy is a boot-shaped country on the continent of Europe. Italy is a peninsula in the Mediterranean Sea. It has an ancient and rich history and many important geographical landmarks including mountains and volcanoes. The capital of Italy is Rome.

Olives:

Olives are small oblong fruits with a hard center pit. They grow on trees in Mediterranean regions. The trees do not grow from seeds, but must be grafted from a branch or root of an existing tree. Olives are primarily used to make oil for cooking. Olive tree wood is commonly used for cooking utensils.

Venice:

Venezia or Venice is an ancient island city in northeastern Italy connected by a series of canals. Venice is famous for its canals and 400 bridges, Saint Mark's Cathedral and Square, carnival, long boats called gondolas and glass making, including mirrors.

The Grand Canal as seen from a gondola boat.

Kilometer:

A kilometer is a unit of length in the metric system. It is shorter than a mile. One kilometer is equal to 1000 meters or 0.62 miles.

Dolomite Mountains:

The Dolomite Mountains are in northeastern Italy and are part of the southern Alps. Because of the mineral, dolomite, the rocks of the mountains have a pale or often white color.

Medieval Superstitions in Europe:

Mirrors were very expensive in medieval times; therefore, it was very unfortunate if one broke. Some people believed that breaking a mirror brought seven years of bad luck. The number thirteen was considered an unlucky number. One explanation was that thirteen people attended the Last Supper, which resulted in the arrest of Jesus. Black cats were considered common companions of witches and causes for bad luck if the cat walked in front of a person.

Cuckoo Birds:

The Common Cuckoo is a medium-size song-bird with a flute like call used to designate territory or to attract a mate. The birds live in trees and eat insects. In neighboring Germany, cuckoos are carved on wooden pendulum clocks. Every hour, a small wooden cuckoo bird emerges through a shuttered window and makes the cuckoo sound to count the number of the new hour.

Persimmon:

Persimmons are light orange round fruits about the size of an apple. The skin and pulp are edible. Persimmons are ripe in the autumn.

Polenta

Polenta is made from boiled cornmeal. It is commonly served in northern Italy as a side dish.

Chicken Wine Pitchers

The Italian chicken pitcher originates from the Renaissance period. A rich man, Giuliano Medicis, was staying in a town near Florence when he evaded assassination because chickens in the yard alerted and woke his guards during a nighttime invasion. The rich man was so grateful to be alive he commissioned craftsmen to produce chicken-shaped wine pitchers. He gave the pitchers to the townspeople. Today, chicken pitchers are traditional gifts to protect a home from danger and intruders.

Befana

According to Italian folklore when the three wise men traveled to visit baby Jesus they met Befana, a witch, who was too busy cleaning her house to accompany them. After the kings left her home, she regretted her decision. She flew on her broom looking for the kings and for Jesus. Unfortunately, she never found them. Now every year on January 6th, Epiphany, she flies on her broom to deliver toys to good boys and girls.

Andrà Tutto Bene

"Andrà Tutto Bene" means "everything will be fine." In 2020 when the COVID-19 virus forced Italy into a very strict lockdown, children made *Andrà Tutto Bene* posters

with rainbows. They displayed the signs outside their windows or on their balconies to give their neighbors hope and encouragement. Many signs are still hanging today.

Photo Credit: Sarah Wells

Fogolar Friulano

A traditional round, open-hearth oven in the Friuli Venezia Giulia region of Italy characterized by a high dome hood under a chimney. This fireplace was common in the 18th century and used both for cooking and heating.

Acknowledgements

Grazie mille God for giving me a gift with words. Thank you for sending Lucky to be our friend, saving him last May and for seeing us through the many trials of his adoption and life in Italy since the summer of 2019. Thank you for using this story to heal and encourage me. Luna and Fortuna have brought me great joy. I pray they will do the same for my readers.

Thank you friends and family who read drafts of this story and gave me feedback. Thank you Mom, Anne Sloop, for enthusiastically messaging me or calling me every time I shared a book update. Thank you James and Daniel for graciously listening every time I was eager to read out loud and for listening to all the other silly stories I've made up through the years to entertain and distract you when you are upset. Thank you Mark for believing in my creativity and for encouraging me to follow through on my dream of publishing this book. Thank you Uncle Dan Dye for agreeing to be my illustrator. Your pictures are joyful and they add magic to this tale! Thank you Michelle

Simpson for answering my questions and coaching me through my first KDP experience. Thank you Graziano Facchini for inviting me inside your home to see "Luna's" fogolar. I hope your family enjoys this story inspired in part by your grandmother's house.

And last, but not least, *grazie* Lucky for being the best *piccolo gatto nero d'Italia;* without you this story would not exist.

Love, Katy

Lucky Roberts, the real Fortuna.

About the Illustrator

Dan Dye is the author's uncle, and he is honored to illustrate her book. Dan is from Chapel Hill, North Carolina and he has a degree in Sociology from the University of North Carolina at Chapel Hill. Dan has enjoyed art since early childhood. In high school and college he nurtured his talents for painting and silversmithing. After retiring from a long career in sales, Dan made silversmithing his second career. He lives in Raleigh, N.C. with his wife of fifty years. They have two daughters and two granddaughters. Through the years they have owned several black cats.

www.dandye.com

About the Author

Photo Credit: Reyna Truscott

Katy Sloop Roberts is from Charlottesville, Virginia and she has a degree in English from the University of North Carolina at Chapel Hill and a master's degree in Physical Therapy from the University of Alabama at Birmingham. Katy has enjoyed writing since her grandparents gave her a lined journal at age seven. "Mario and The Stones" is her first book. As an Air Force spouse, she has lived in many U.S. states, Germany and Italy. Katy lives in Aviano, Italy with her husband, two sons, and a black cat named Lucky. Katy is writing a memoir about her family's friendship and adoption of Lucky in 2020.

ksrobertspt@gmail.com

Made in the USA
Monee, IL
10 September 2021